LUNACORN

Rachel DeCarlo
Illustrated by Jess Burbank

*Dedicated to the real Luna May and my daughter, Sofia, who came
up with the idea for this book. May you continue to dream big.*

For inquiries, please contact Lunacornbook@gmail.com.

Printed in the United States of America
First Printing: October 2023

Library of Congress Control Number: 2023915122
ISBN: 979-8-218-24590-0 (Paperback)
ISBN: 979-8-218-24591-7 (eBook)

Cover design by Jess Burbank
Interior layout and formatting by Jess Burbank
Main text set in Baskerville. Cover text set in Coffee Scrawl.
The artwork was created in watercolor, gouache, colored pencil, and collage.

I am grateful to and for:

Mama and Papa T, for the confidence and courage
they instilled in me; Paul for his silly character voices
that make reading children's books fun; my twin sister,
Megan for her proofing and industry expertise;
and to all my other friends and family that supported
the creation of this little book.

I have the cutest, sweetest, most wonderfullest black dog in Seattle—Luna May. If you get too close to her, she will lick you—your hands, your shirt that still smells of lunch, or your stinky feet.

Now she's almost seven and starting to get old with a bit of gray fur around her mouth, and she can't catch up to me like she used to.

Today Daddy and I are sitting on the floor rubbing Luna's belly. When she lies on her back, perfectly still, we like to sing a certain song and pretend to play bongos on her tummy.

"Do do do do do, puppy bongo." She loves this.

Suddenly, the doorbell rings and Daddy says, "Must be that present for Luna's birthday." I have been excited about this day for soooo long—Luna May's seventh birthday party. There is going to be a bone-shaped birthday cake and a squirrel piñata.

When my dad leaves the room, I notice a blue flashing light on the wall in my bedroom. It is faint at first and then seems to get bigger and brighter.

As I get closer to the light, I see it is coming from an opening in a tiny door, barely bigger than my hand. A fairy door? I'm sure it wasn't there before. I get on my hands and knees to take a closer look. Now I hear a humming, like fairies singing, calling me to come closer. I know Luna sees this too as she starts to bark. I gently pet her to comfort her. As I move closer, I start to feel a pull toward the door. Then poof … we shrink and are sucked in through the door.

   I find myself swirling around in what feels like a windstorm. I can
see a rush of green light. The air smells like dirt and fresh-cut leaves.
My curls are flying around my head, getting all in my eyes and mouth,
and my body is being tossed around. I feel something furry brush my
arm. A tail? I hear a frantic Luna bark.

I land wobbly, alone in a park. Not just any park—Seward Park near my house. I know it's Seward because my family takes Luna there almost every weekend. It pokes out into sparkling blue Lake Washington dotted with sailboats.

There are so many evergreen trees with fancy names my parents have told me before, but I can never remember: Douglas *sir* and *sticker* spruce? There are windy trails, rocky beaches, and sometimes a bald eagle if you're lucky.

I'm standing near a long stretch of beach, by a red fire hydrant Luna likes to pee on. It feels like Seward Park, but not. Everything is covered by a shimmery mist. The sun is a bright yellow pineapple with sunglasses. The grass smells strongly of playdough. And whoa—blue ice cream cones are growing from bushes. I hesitate but then lick one. Maximum sweetness!

In the distance, I hear a "ruff!" Luna! I was so distracted, I completely forgot about her. I yell her name as loudly as I can, "Lunnna!" My voice bounces off the trees. Is my voice louder here?

At this point, Luna—at least, I think it's Luna—pops out of some salmonberry bushes. She is still furry with white patches on her chest, but she seems more puppylike, springy, with no gray hair on her chin, and instead of her normal black fur, she has bright rainbow-colored stripes.

Also, she's not just a dog anymore. She has a polka dot *horn* coming from her head that blinks purple and a fluffy rainbow-colored horsey tail. Could she be a unicorn? I love unicorns—those mythical horned beasts from all my fairy tales. But no—this is not a unicorn, and it's not Luna.

It's a

LUNACORN!

Lunacorn can do some strange things ... she gently puts me on her back to give me a piggyback ride and winks when she puts me down.

But then, even more shocking, she surprises herself—and me— by speaking human. It comes out first like a whisper and then a more confident, deep unicorn-like voice.

"Whooooa!" she said, touching her throat with a paw. "Did I say that? Sofia. Wait ... I can say your name!"

My jaw drops.

"I have so much I want to tell you! First, my favorite dog bone has been under your bookshelf for months, and I'd appreciate it if you got it for me when we get home. Second, thanks for always giving me your leftovers under the table. Third, you are my favorite little human, and I love you."

My heart thumps and
I smile from ear to ear and
give Lunacorn a big hug.

We frolic around the park giggling, enjoying
Lunacorn's new tricks and the wonders of the park.
She runs at top speed like she used to...

and when I do her favorite tummy rub, her belly turns into an actual bongo!

She licks me as she always does, but the lick turns to gold glitter.

Later, we see orcas playing cards on the beach, smiling at us with their wide mouths ...

and then we get caught in confetti rain
that sticks to my skin and her fur.

After a while, we see a dock through
the mist with what looks like a salmon
with a fishing rod sitting on the side,
whistling a tune.

When it hears us coming, it claps its fins together in excitement and yells, "Hi, friends! Are you lost?"

"I guess we are," I say. "How are we going to get back to the birthday party?"

"Don't worry," says the fish. "You just need to follow Lunacorn's horn to find the key to get back home. It flashes purple when you are getting closer. I suggest you go that way," it says, pointing the way we just came.

We thank the friendly salmon and turn around.
Now that we know what to do, we move quickly.
We go a few steps down the path. Lunacorn's horn
is a light purple at first and then it gets darker and
darker. We cut through the park's maze of paths
shaded by big trees with leaves the size of steering
wheels protecting us from the pineapple sun that
shimmers everywhere.

Eventually, we come to a playground I thought I had been to a gazillion times but this one was, well … rad. It had a floating turtle seesaw that hovered over the ground, a web of underground passageways, and overground tunnels connected by bridges, tree forts, and a few old-looking tugboats that remind me of ones I have seen on Lake Union.
I pause our key-finding for a few minutes and play.

After I land yelling at the top of my lungs from a two-story slide, I notice what is usually a sandpit, filled with chocolate sauce. As Luna and I approach, her horn starts to chirp and gets louder and louder.

A heart-shaped rock with a glittery pink key is in the middle of the pit.

Luna yells excitedly, "Let me fetch it. I never get to eat chocolate at home!" She jumps in and slowly paddles to the key, lapping up the chocolate on the way and barking in delight.

When Luna climbs out of the chocolate swamp, she shakes it off, just like she does at home, and gets chocolate all over me. We both giggle, snorting chocolate from our noses.

She drops the key and in front of us, a tree as big as the Space Needle appears out of nowhere with a door and keyhole made for this pink glittery key. I put it in the slot and a trumpet plays. The door opens and beyond is the real world.

I hug Lunacorn. "You'll probably change back to a regular dog, you know."

Lunacorn's eyes are bright. She's always happy, no matter what. "That's okay," she says giving me a lick, "I'll still remember. It's time to go home."

I hold on to her colorful mane and we swoosh back through the whirling green tunnel and land gently on my pillow fort in my room.

My mommy walks in and says, "Oh, there you two are. We are about to start the fun. Come on."

After giving Luna all her treats, I say, "I have one more surprise for Lunacorn."

Everyone looks at me strangely.

"Oh, I mean Luna May."

After she's been chewing for a while, she looks up at me and winks.

Made in United States
Troutdale, OR
10/09/2023